NO FRIENDS

by JAMES STEVENSON

GREENWILLOW BOOKS, NEW YORK

Black pen and watercolors were used to prepare the full-color art. The typeface is Clearface.

Printed in Hong Kong by South China Printing Co.   First Edition   1 2 3 4 5 6 7 8 9 10

Library of Congress Cataloging-in-Publication Data

Stevenson, James, (date)   No friends.   Summary: Worried that they won't make friends in their new neighborhood, Mary Ann and Louie listen to Grandpa reminisce about the new friends he made when he moved to another neighborhood.   [1. Moving, Household—Fiction.   2. Friendship—Fiction] I. Title. PZ7.S8474No 1986   [E]   85-27247   ISBN 0-688-06506-6   ISBN 0-688-06507-4 (lib. bdg.)

"Hello, Mary Ann! Hello, Louie!" said Grandpa.

"Hi, Grandpa!" said Mary Ann.

"Did you come to see our new house, Grandpa?" asked Louie.

"I certainly did! How do you like your new neighborhood?" asked Grandpa.

"The neighborhood was cold and ugly.

The streets were icy, and the wind was always blowing . . .

in different directions."

"It was so lonely that Wainey and I talked to our reflections in the ice."

"I was told there was a boy named Franklyn— but he lived miles away. One day we went to see him."

"Every day Wainey and I went riding on my bike looking for friends. One day a kid ran by."

"Wainey and I raced home and stayed inside for two days.

Then we went out very carefully.

We didn't see any children but we saw strange signs on the walls and fences.

We came around a corner . . .

On the way home, we ran into the tough kids we'd met in the winter."

"I ran after Wainey.
Soon I began to hear sounds of
crashes up and down the streets.

I kept trying to catch him, but
every time I saw Wainey he was
on less bike . . ."

"Finally the last wheel came rolling
around one corner—without Wainey.

Then, suddenly, Wainey came sailing by.

Wainey bounced through the town.

Gradually, he bounced into our neighborhood.

He did a final somersault, jackknife, and swan dive . . .

and landed in the birdbath on our lawn.

Then Wally and Prince and all the children
came up on our porch and we all had some lemonade."